Fashion Fairy Princess

Thanks fairy much Catherine Coe!

First published in the UK in 2014 by Scholastic Children's Books
An imprint of Scholastic Ltd
Euston House, 24 Eversholt Street
London, NW1 1DB, UK
Registered office: Westfield Road, Southam, Warwickshire, CV47 0RA
SCHOLASTIC and associated logos are trademarks and/or registered
trademarks of Scholastic Inc.

ISBN 978 1407 14588 4

A CIP catalogue record for this book is available from the British Library.

Printed and bound by CPI Group (UK) Ltd, Croydon, CR0 4YY
Papers used by Scholastic Children's Books are made
from wood grown in sustainable forests.

1 3 5 7 9 10 8 6 4 2

This is a work of fiction. Names, characters, places,
incidents and dialogues are products of the author's imagination
or are used fictitiously. Any resemblance to actual people, living
or dead, events or locales is entirely coincidental.

www.scholastic.co.uk
www.fashionfairyprincess.com

Fashion Fairy Princess

Pip

in Jewel Forest

POPPY COLLINS

SCHOLASTIC

Dream
Mountain

Jewel Forest

Sparkle
City

Star
Valley

River
Sapphire

Shimmer Island

Glitter Ocean

Welcome to the world of the
fashion fairy princesses! Join Pip
and friends on their magical adventures
in fairyland.

They can't wait to explore

Jewel Forest!

Can you?

Chapter 1

Toadstool Town Hall in Jewel Forest hummed with the chatter of fairies as they waited for the meeting to begin. The town hall was an impressive circular building deep in the magical forest. The walls were made entirely of gemstones, which let light flow in from outside, even though there were no windows.

Pip, Willa, Catkin and Blossom sat next to each other on red-and-white toadstool seats, waiting for someone to appear on the stage in the centre of the hall.

"I wonder what this is all about," said Willa as she adjusted her sycamore hairband in her long dark hair. "I hope there isn't something wrong in the forest!"

"Maybe it's something good," Pip said in her tiny fairy voice. Pip was the smallest of all of her friends, and she had a voice to match.

"Well, it can't be a celebration," added Blossom, who owned the bakery in Jewel Forest, "because I haven't been asked to bake a special cake!"

"Oh look, it's the mayor," whispered Catkin. She nodded her head at the stage, making her red curly hair bounce about.

A large yellow frog hopped along one of the aisles and on to the stage. He wore a smart red waistcoat that sparkled with ruby jewels.

Ribbit, he said into the bellflower microphone on the stage. "Is this microphone working?" *Ribbit!*

The audience was a sea of bobbing heads as everyone nodded at the same time.

"Good. Then I will begin," said the mayor in his deep, croaky, froggy voice. "Thank you for gathering here today. I have an important announcement that I think you will all find very exciting indeed."

"Ooh, I wonder what it will be!" whispered Blossom.

"I am delighted to tell you all that. . ." The mayor paused as everyone sat forward on their seats – "Jewel Forest is to host the next Fairy Olympics!"

Hearing these words, everyone in Toadstool Town Hall cheered. The Fairy Olympics were held every four years – but Jewel Forest had never hosted them before. It was a *really* big deal.

"This is BRILLIANT!" cried Willa as she fluttered her wings in excitement.

"Oh, I can't wait!" added Catkin, clapping her hands. She turned to Pip.

"You were right – it *is* something good!"

But although her friends were delighted, Pip wasn't so sure. The little fairy didn't really like sports – and she wasn't very good at them!

Ribbit! croaked the mayor as he tried to quieten the audience. "Now, creatures of the forest, there's a great deal of work to do! The Fairy Olympics will take place in just two days' time, so we'll need lots of help to get everything ready. And you'll need to practise for the events, as we'll have fairies visiting from all over fairyland to compete in our Olympics. We'll put on a fantastic show for the forest animals and creatures! There will be events designed especially for the forest: Toadstool Trampolining, Branch Gymnastics, River Rafting and Fairy Relay."

The mayor grinned and clapped his

webbed hands together. "Right, that's all. Thank you, fairies! I know we're going to put on an Olympics like no other, and that you'll do Jewel Forest proud!"

Everyone began fluttering out of the hall. "You go on without me," Catkin told her friends. "I want to speak to the mayor about being on the organizing committee."

The fairies grinned – if there was one thing Catkin loved to do above all else, it was organize!

The fairy friends waved goodbye to Catkin as they walked through the grand town hall entrance. Outside were two golden statues: one of a princess fairy and one of a hummingbird, showing the harmony between the fairies and creatures of the forest.

They emerged into the lush green forest, which sparkled in the afternoon sunshine. The jewels hanging from the trees glistened and the shiny leaves gleamed.

"I'm so looking forward to the Branch Gymnastics," said Blossom. "It's my favourite sport!"

The three fairies stepped on to the

fairy skyway. The skyway was high above the forest ground and made of leafy bridges that connected the tree houses and shops. Shiny gems, dotted between the leaves, meant that it always glittered, even at night!

"I love Toadstool Trampolining!" said Willa. "I'm a bit rusty, but if I start practising right away, I hope I'll get the hang of it again quickly."

"Oh, and what about the River Rafting?" said Blossom, spinning round to face her friends. "It sounds like so much fun!"

The friends continued to chatter as they fluttered back home, although Pip was quiet. A niggling thought buzzed about her head: *What am I going to do? I really don't like sports!*

· · ● Chapter 2 ◗ · ·

With just two days until the Fairy
Olympics, everyone immediately set to
work. The whole forest buzzed with
excitement about the Olympics, and
the fairies and creatures flitted about
madly, all helping to prepare for the
big day.

The next morning, Pip bumped into
Catkin on her way to Blossom's bakery.
"Oh, hi, Catkin!" She waved at the

red-headed fairy flying towards her on the fairy skyway. "How are things going?"

Catkin held out a piece of reed paper. "There's so much to do — I've got to sort out the seating, the refreshments for the competitors *and* the medals and podium!" Despite this, Catkin had a big smile across her face. "But I love it — this Fairy Olympics is going to be the best *ever*!"

"With you in charge, I'm sure it will be!" said Pip. "Would you like anything from Blossom's bakery? I'm just going to pick up a ruby-jam tart."

"Not right now, thanks — but say hello from me!"

"Of course!" Pip squeaked in her little voice.

Pip zoomed through the crowd of fairies on the skyway. Being small meant

she could easily weave left and right, up
and down, past everyone.

Back in her pretty tree house, Pip
waited for the tea to brew and thought
about the Olympics. *How will I ever keep
up with the bigger, stronger fairies?* She
poured a cup of steaming beechnut tea
and took a sip. Usually, tea and a tart
would calm her down, but today they

didn't help at all. Pip worried that the whole forest would laugh at her when they saw how bad she was at sports.

She put down her mug and sat forward in her acorn seat. "There's nothing else for it," she told herself. "I'll just have to practise!"

That night, when most of the fairies in Jewel Forest were sleeping soundly in their tree homes, Pip crept quietly through her arched doorway and into the darkening forest. She fluttered along the skyway towards the forest floor.

Luckily, the sparkling gems along the bridges lit up the way – together with the light from the crescent moon above. Pip heard the flap of jewel moths' wings and the hoot of owls as she flew quietly past. She'd never been out in the forest by herself at night before, but it didn't feel scary. In fact, it felt more magical than ever.

Pip headed for the base of the silver-leaf willow, a large, drooping tree with leaves made entirely of silver. It was surrounded by hundreds of white-spotted purple toadstools – perfect for practising Toadstool Trampolining.

She gently flapped her wings to rise up on to a toadstool. Balancing lightly on the toadstool, she then slowly curled up her wings.

"OK, now try a little jump," Pip told

herself. She bent her knees, took a breath and leapt up – but as she landed, her feet slipped from the top of the toadstool and she slid down the side and into the moss below.

"Come on, Pip – get up and try again!" she said to herself as she stood up and dusted down her purple leggings.

But time and time again, Pip fell off the toadstool. *I'm going to make such a fairy-fool of myself!* she thought. Pip was fluttering back on to the toadstool for the tenth time when she heard a flap and a

flitter. But these weren't a bat's wings —
they were too quiet for that. Who was
there?

She squinted in the gloom and saw
the shape of a fairy appear. *Willa!
What's she doing here in the middle of the
night?*

"Hello!" Willa called. "Who's that over
there?"

Pip gave Willa a little wave. "It's me,
Pip," she said.

Willa frowned and fluttered nearer. Her
big brown eyes were wide with surprise.
"Pip — what in fairyland are you doing
here at this time?"

"I'm . . . I'm. . ." Pip didn't know what
to say. "I . . . I couldn't sleep. What are *you*
doing here?" she said, changing the subject.

Willa fluttered on to a nearby toadstool
and began jumping. Pip stared in

amazement — it was as if Willa's feet were connected to the toadstool with elastic! "I wanted to practise my triple backspins in peace — it's always so crowded here in the daytime."

Pip sat down on her toadstool and, with her face cupped in her hands, watched Willa jump, spin and flip. "You're FANTASTIC," she said to her friend. "I wish I was half as good as you."

Willa stopped bouncing and looked at Pip. "But if you practise, I'm sure you'll soon get better at it. It's not that difficult." Willa did a pirouette on her toadstool as if to show her. "See!"

"No, Willa – you don't understand. I'm *really* bad at it," Pip confided. "I can't even do a simple jump without falling off." To demonstrate, Pip tried to bounce on the toadstool for the eleventh time and fell straight to the floor.

"How about I help you?" Willa offered. "I could give you some pointers."

But no matter how much Willa tried to help Pip, the little fairy couldn't get the hang of Toadstool Trampolining. Over and over again she tried. And over and over again, Pip had to pick herself up from the mossy ground.

"Please don't worry," Willa said, when Pip decided it was time she got to bed. "I'm sure there's something you're good at – we just have to find out what!"

Chapter 3

Pip was still in bed when she heard a knock on the door the next morning. She rubbed her eyes and blinked at the early dawn light that flooded in through the sapphire windows.

She climbed out of her palm-leaf hammock and fluttered over to open the door.

"Oh, hi, Blossom!" Pip greeted her friend in her gentle voice. "You're up early!"

"Oh, I'm always up early – to bake! But actually, I've given myself the day off today. I'm here to help you!"

Pip frowned. "What do you mean?"

Blossom grinned and her green eyes twinkled. "I've come to help you learn Branch Gymnastics!"

Pip's heart sank to the tips of her fairy toes. "Did Willa tell you about last night?" she asked.

"Well, er, yes," replied Blossom. "We all want to do everything we can to help!"

Pip shook her head. "It's so embarrassing that I can't do sports. And however hard I try, I just don't like them!" She fought back tears, thinking about how terrible she'd been at the Toadstool Trampolining.

Blossom reached her arms out and gave

her friend a hug. "But there's no harm in having a go, is there?"

Deep down Pip knew that her friends were just being nice. And maybe they *could* help her get a bit better. "All right," she said. "Do you mind waiting while I change into some sports clothes? I can't do gymnastics in my pyjamas!"

Soon Pip was wearing a butterfly-print T-shirt with spider-silk black leggings. "Let's go!" she said cheerily, trying to be upbeat about practising – even though it was the last thing she wanted to do.

Blossom led Pip along the fairy skyway to a tree branch in a quiet corner of Jewel Forest. "I often come to train here," she told Pip. "No one ever disturbs me, and these topaz trees have really smooth branches – perfect to swing and spin on!"

Pip looked around at the forest. The light-blue topaz gems glittered on the leaves of the trees, casting a magical light everywhere. It looked so peaceful, and despite it being dawn, Pip couldn't even hear a bird singing. Not that she didn't enjoy birdsong – but she needed total concentration if she was ever going to get better at sports!

"Come and sit next to me, Pip," called Blossom. She was perched on a short branch near the bottom of the tree with her legs dangling. "We can do some basics together."

Pip fluttered down on to the branch next to her friend.

Blossom let her legs slip off the branch so she hung by her arms. "This is the Dangle Pose," she said. "That's how a lot of Branch Gymnastics moves begin."

Pip looked down at her own arms. She wasn't sure they'd be strong enough to hold her — even though she didn't weigh much.

"Now, I'll show you a few moves. Watch me carefully. . ."

Pip sat on the branch while Blossom moved her legs back and forth to start swinging. She soon built up enough momentum to swing forward, over the top of the branch and around, then around again, and again. Her wavy blonde hair billowed out in the breeze as she spun faster and faster. Blossom became almost a blur, and Pip wondered how in fairyland she'd ever do that. Surely it would make her really dizzy?

Blossom suddenly let go of the branch, did a double backwards somersault in the air and landed back on the branch on her feet.

Pip couldn't help but clap. "That was incredible! But I'll never be able to do anything like that. . ."

Blossom sat down. "Well, how about we start with a spin? It's the most basic move in Branch Gymnastics. What do you think?"

Pip nodded slowly. "OK . . . I guess it can't hurt to try." How hard could it be? Blossom made it look easy, at least.

Blossom slipped back down to the Dangle Pose and kicked her legs forward to swing herself to and fro. Pip tried to copy her, but instead of swinging smoothly like Blossom, she just sort of . . . wriggled about. *I look more like a caterpillar than a gymnast!* Pip thought to herself.

"Keep going," Blossom said encouragingly. "Bend your knees, then straighten them out again — that will help you swing."

Pip did as Blossom said, but although her legs were moving up and down, her body stayed still. What's more, her arms were really aching from dangling for so long!

"You can do it," said Blossom, but as Pip tried kicking out again, she lost her grip on the branch. She tumbled downwards, and had to quickly unfurl her wings before

she hit the ground. She fluttered them out just in time, but rather than flying up towards Blossom, Pip zoomed off, away from the topaz trees.

"I can't do it," Pip called over her shoulder, tears in her eyes. "I'll never be good at sports. There's just no point in trying!"

"Pip, where are you going?" Blossom called after her friend. But Pip had already disappeared among the trees of Jewel Forest.

Chapter 4

I shouldn't have flown away, thought Pip
as she sat on the banks of the River
Sapphire. *Blossom was only trying to
help.* She picked up a pearl-pebble and
skimmed it across the shimmering water.
When they were younger, the fairy
friends had often played here, seeing who
could skim their pebble the furthest.

"Pip!" called Blossom. "Are you OK?"

Pip jumped at the sudden shout.

Blossom fluttered over until she was standing on the grassy riverbank beside Pip. Even the grass was special in Jewel Forest – it glistened with crystal dewdrops.

"I'm sorry I made you do gymnastics," began Blossom.

Pip looked up at her friend. "Oh, please don't be sorry, Blossom! You were just being kind and trying to teach me. I'm sorry for flying away!" She fiddled with a pebble she had in her hand. "It's just that I'm *never* going to be good at sports – I'm too tiny. And the Fairy Olympics are tomorrow. Everyone's going to laugh at me!"

Blossom put an arm around her friend. "No one will laugh at you, Pip. You know the Fairy Olympics are all about taking part – not winning!"

As Blossom spoke she heard a splashing coming along the river. She glanced up to see a dinghy filled with forest fairies. "Oh look, they must be practising for the River Rafting!" Blossom had a sudden thought. "Hey, Pip, have you ever tried rafting? I bet being small doesn't make a difference with that!"

But the idea of being in the river made Pip tremble. "You're right, Blossom. But do you remember that time when we were much younger, and I fell into the river? We'd been skimming pearl-pebbles near Garnet Gorge, and I reached out too far and toppled off the bank. . ."

Blossom gasped. How could she have forgotten that! Pip had been terrified – she hadn't yet learnt to swim, and the current had tugged at her wings and pulled her under the water. She was lucky that a water vole had heard the commotion, and popped out of his hole nearby. He'd saved her just in time.

"Of course – I should've remembered." Poor Pip. They'd all been really scared that day.

"It's not that I don't like the river... I love being near it and listening to the soothing sound of the rushing water. I just don't like being *in* it!"

"I'm not surprised," said Blossom sympathetically. She and Pip sat in silence for a while, watching the ripples on the pink water circle across the river.

The peace was broken by a familiar voice. "Hello, Pip! Hello, Blossom!" The two fairies turned round to see Catkin flying over to them.

"Oh, hi, Catkin!" said Pip, putting on a brave face. "How's the organizing going?"

Catkin grinned. "I'm on my way to collect the medals," she told them. "The tree squirrels have been making them. What are you two up to?"

"Oh, er, just hanging out," said Blossom. She thought Pip might not want to tell Catkin about her sports disaster.

But Pip wanted to be honest. "Actually, we're here because Blossom was trying to teach me Branch Gymnastics. But I was terrible and flew off, and Blossom came to find me. The truth is, Catkin, I'm really worried about the Olympics tomorrow," she admitted.

Catkin sat down next to Pip. "Oh, Pip, please don't worry. You're good at other things, like sewing, and dancing – and you're an amazing singer. Not every fairy can be good at sports!"

Pip gave Catkin a small smile. "Thanks,

Catkin. But the thought of competing tomorrow makes me feel sick."

"I've got an idea!" said Catkin, bouncing up and pulling at Pip's hand to do the same. "Come and help me with the last-minute organization. There's still so much to do – I promise it'll take your mind off it!"

"That sounds great," said Pip. "If you're sure I won't get in the way?"

"Of course not – it'll be brilliant to have an extra pair of wings!"

Pip and Catkin worked non-stop for the rest of the day. First, they picked up the medals from the tree squirrels. They'd made them out of gold, silver and bronze conkers tied with spider-silk thread. The gorgeous medals glistened in a wicker basket, and Pip couldn't help but feel a stab of disappointment that there was no chance of her winning one.

But there was no time to be sad. Next, Catkin and Pip flew down to Bluebell Clearing, a large mossy patch of ground surrounded by bluebell fields. Catkin explained that this was where most of the events would take place. It was the perfect area, with lots of natural sunlight pouring down, and tree stumps dotted around for the spectators to sit on.

Once they'd sorted out the seats, they had to build the podium and stage. Luckily, Catkin had already asked some sparrows to gather as many golden acorns as they could find. The shiny nutshells were piled up at the centre of the clearing.

"This calls for a little fairy magic," said Catkin. She put a hand into the pocket of her jeans and pulled out a handful of fairy-dust. She tipped some carefully into Pip's outstretched palms. "I always find fairy magic works best if there are two of you," she explained to Pip. "Ready, steady, go!"

Pip and Catkin squeezed their eyes shut and threw the fairy-dust up into the air. They could hear the tinkle of the dust as it landed on the acorn pile. But when Pip

opened her
eyes, the pile
wasn't there
any more –
in its place
was a glittering

golden stage made from shells, with a
winners' podium in the centre!

"Wow, it's beautiful!" cried Pip.

Next, the two friends made the
refreshments for the fairy competitors.
They gathered daisy petals and peaches to
make the daisy-peach punch and poured
it into leaf cups to serve.

The sky had turned a deep purple
colour by the time Catkin announced
that they'd finished. "Thanks *so* much,
Pip – I would've been up all night if I
hadn't had your help!"

"Thanks, Catkin – it really did take

my mind off the sports tomorrow. In fact,
I'm actually looking forward to it – it's
so magical down here, I can't wait to see
everyone's faces!"

Chapter 5

Pip slept soundly that night – she was exhausted after helping Catkin all day. And when she woke up, she didn't feel quite so anxious about the Fairy Olympics. *How bad can it be?* she thought as she made a cup of beechnut tea. *There's no point in worrying about it now.*

She put on a special "Jewel Forest" Olympics T-shirt – something else the organizing committee had taken charge of. On the front was a sparkly leaf made out of tiny crystals.

Pip fluttered along the fairy skyway to Bluebell Clearing. As she got closer, the skyway became busier and the chatter in the air noisier. She gasped when the clearing came into view. It looked so different from yesterday, when it had been empty and quiet. Now it was buzzing with forest creatures waiting for the Olympics to start. On the tree-stump chairs sat every type of forest dweller imaginable – from frogs to fireflies, rabbits to worms, sparrows to spiders. Some held up signs saying "We Love the Jewel Forest Fairies" and "Go for Gold", and Pip even saw a group of rabbits wearing face paints!

In the clearing, hundreds of fairies

stretched and fluttered, and drank cups
of daisy-peach punch. They smiled and
laughed and joked – they didn't look
at all nervous! As well as the fairies Pip
knew, who wore Jewel Forest T-shirts, she
spotted others wearing Star Valley, Sparkle
City and Dream Mountain T-shirts.

Pip suddenly felt terrified. She hadn't
imagined how many creatures would be
here to watch – not to mention all the
other fairies who'd come from outside
Jewel Forest to compete in the Fairy

Olympics. She shrank back behind an elderflower bush. Maybe she could fly back home before anyone saw her and hide for the rest of the day?

"Oh, hi, Pip!" Pip swung round – it was Princess Primrose and her younger sister Nutmeg, also wearing Jewel Forest T-shirts. Pip's princess friends lived in the Tree Palace, which was built into an ancient pink diamond-nut tree in the heart of the forest. "Wow, the Bluebell Clearing looks amazing! Catkin told me you helped her put all the finishing touches to it yesterday."

"Um, yes," said Pip in her tiny voice. "Thank you."

Nutmeg smiled, making the freckles on her cheeks dance about. "It's brilliant. I can't wait for the Olympics to start!"

"We'd better join the others," said

Primrose, "before the mayor's opening speech!"

Primrose linked arms with Pip and the little fairy found herself fluttering down to the clearing. *Well, I can't hide now!* Pip thought to herself.

As the fairies joined their friends before the golden stage, the mayor hopped out in front of the bellflower microphone.

Ribbit! Ribbit! "Hello, everyone! I am thrilled to welcome you all – fairies, animals, insects and other creatures – to the Jewel Forest Fairy Olympics! This is a very exciting day – the first Fairy Olympics to be held in Jewel Forest – and we have some very special events lined up for you!" The mayor paused for a moment and the audience clapped. *Ribbit!* "So, we're going to begin with River Rafting on River Sapphire. Then we have Toadstool Trampolining, followed by Branch Gymnastics. The second-to-last event will be the Fairy Relay. The final event is top secret, and won't be revealed until later!"

Pip looked around at her fairy friends. "A top-secret event? I wonder what it is! Catkin, do you know about it?"

Catkin shrugged her shoulders. "Nope!" she whispered. "It's a surprise to me, too!"

"Please make your way to River Sapphire for the first event!" announced the mayor in his deep, croaky voice.

The fairies were put in teams, competing against the other lands in fairyland. Pip was relieved that she was in the same team as Primrose – she was always so calm. But that didn't stop Pip from squeezing her eyes tightly shut throughout the entire race.

At the front of the raft, Nutmeg's sister yelled for them to go faster as River Sapphire became a sea of splashing oars. Pip's heart thumped, and although she tried to loosen her grip on the sides to

pick up her oars, she just couldn't – she was too scared.

"There's the finish line!" called Nutmeg after what seemed like hours, but was probably only a few minutes.

Pip didn't dare look, but seconds later she heard the mayor announce that a team from Dream Mountain had won. Then she felt Primrose's arms around her, helping guide her out of the boat and on to dry land.

Thank fairyland that's over, thought Pip, finally daring to open her eyes as she fluttered to the bank. She hoped to the tips of her fairy wings the other events wouldn't be quite as bad as that one.

Chapter 6

After the River Rafting medal ceremony, the mayor announced the next event: Toadstool Trampolining.

Pip's heart sank, remembering just how bad she'd been when she'd tried to practise. In Bluebell Clearing, she looked around nervously at all the larger fairies lined up behind toadstools. Pip went to find her own, and was relieved to discover a spare one right at the back.

It was lower and smaller than the other toadstools – perfect for her!

The audience watched as the fairies stood waiting for the signal from the mayor. "Fairies, this event is all about how high you can bounce! Remember, if you fall off, you're out of the competition." He held up his palm-leaf flag. "And, ready, steady . . . GO!"

Pip fluttered up on to her toadstool, tucked in her wings, and kept her feet steady. She glanced around – some of the other fairies were already bouncing up and down expertly. She could see Willa, in the front row of toadstools, jumping away. Her silky long black hair flowed up and down as she moved through the air.

"OK, here goes," Pip said silently. She bent her knees, took a deep breath,

and jumped. The toadstool wobbled
under her, and although she tried to
land with her little feet balanced, her left
foot slipped and she found herself sliding
down the toadstool. She managed a smile
as she landed on the soft mossy ground.
Oh well, at least that's over quickly!

Pip watched the rest of the Toadstool
Trampolining with her friends – all of
them except Willa were out of the event.

Soon there were only three fairies
left: Willa, Goldie – also from Jewel
Forest – and Fern, from Star Valley.
The audience cheered them on as they
bounced higher and higher, their faces
straight with concentration. Pip gasped as
Willa somersaulted in the air, and clapped
her hands hard as she landed perfectly
on the toadstool. Goldie then tried to
do the same, but as she spun in the air
she drifted to the side, and found it
impossible to land back on her toadstool.
Now there were just two fairies left!

Willa launched herself upwards into a
backflip. Pip held her breath – this was
the highest she'd bounced so far – but as
Willa landed she tipped backwards. Her
arms flailed about as she tried to regain
her balance, but it was no good – Willa
tumbled off the toadstool.

"I'm so sorry you didn't win, Willa,"
said Pip when her friend came to join
them after receiving her silver conker
medal.

Willa smiled. "It's my own fault – I
shouldn't have shown off so much!
Anyway, I'm really pleased to be second – I
didn't even think I had a chance of
winning a medal!"

RIBBIT! RIBBIT! RIBBIT! boomed the mayor, silencing the chattering crowd. "Next is Branch Gymnastics. Fairy contestants, take your places, please."

But there aren't any branches nearby! thought Pip. "What does he mean?" she asked Willa.

Her friend pointed towards the cherry-jewel tree on one side of the clearing. A golden branch began to grow out of its trunk, slowly making its way across the Bluebell Clearing.

"We've got a bit of fairy magic for this event!" said the mayor. "Look out for the branch, everyone!"

It continued to stretch across the whole length of the clearing, right in front of the seated spectators.

"Wow!" said Pip.

"It's wonderful, isn't it?" said Catkin.

"We had to collect a lot of fairy-dust to create that magic!"

Soon, the fairies were all lined up on the branch. "You will have fifty puffs of a dandelion clock to show us what you can do. At the end, the audience will vote for the winner!"

Pip couldn't help but shake with fear as she sat between Nutmeg and Blossom, her legs hanging nervously from the branch.

"And . . . GO!" croaked the mayor as he started blowing on the dandelion he held.

While many of the other fairies began swinging expertly on the golden branch, Pip lowered herself down slowly, until she dangled by her hands. She knew she had to at least try, so she bent her legs, as Blossom had shown her. Then she caught sight of Blossom out of the corner of her eye, performing triple cartwheels. *She's unbelievable!* thought Pip.

"Ten puffs left!" the mayor told them. The audience's cheers grew louder as they encouraged the fairies. But Pip still couldn't even swing herself back and forth. She looked along the line of contestants – every single one of them was swinging, even if some weren't quite flipping over the branch. Everyone was better than her!

"Three . . . two . . . one . . . and stop!" called the mayor. Pip fluttered to the ground. She was just glad that was over — and that the audience seemed to be so impressed by the other fairies' acrobatics, they hadn't noticed how terrible she was!

To decide on the winner, the mayor told the audience to blow on a dandelion clock while thinking of their favourite fairy gymnast. It was a magical sight as the dandelion seeds then flew out of the audience's hands — or paws — and came to rest at the feet of their chosen fairy. Pip wasn't surprised she didn't get a single dandelion seed, but was thrilled when she saw the pile in front of Blossom.

"Blossom, you're the clear winner!" announced the mayor.

The blonde fairy stared down at her

pile of dandelion seeds and blinked
repeatedly, as if she
couldn't believe it.

"Well done,
Blossom!" said Pip,
giving her friend
a huge hug. "I'm
so pleased for
you." And Pip
really meant
it — she was
delighted for

her friend, even if she didn't have a hope
of winning a medal of her own!

Chapter 7

Blossom still looked dazed as the mayor hung her winner's golden conker over her head and the whole forest cheered.

"I can't believe it!" she said to her friends as the fairies drank daisy-peach punch. "I've never won anything before!"

Primrose put an arm around her friend's shoulders. "You were miles better than anyone else – I've never seen such complicated spins and flips!"

As the fairies finished their drinks, the mayor announced the next event: Fairy Relay. "This will rely on everyone in a team to fly as fast as they can."

The mayor picked out the leaders of each team, who then had to pick their team members. Pip's stomach whirled with embarrassment – of course no one would want to pick her! For the second time that day, she wished she could hide away.

Fairy names were called out one after the other as the teams gathered together, and soon all Pip's friends had disappeared from her side. She stared at her feet, not even able to glance at the stage. Finally Pip realized it was just her left, as she heard her name being called

out by Poppy,
another Jewel
Forest fairy.
She rushed
over to join
the team, her
head down,
her cheeks
burning
with shame.

"Fairies,
please line up on the ground in front
of the cherry-chestnut tree at the far end
of the Bluebell Clearing."

Pip let out a little sigh. At least there
was only one more event left.

"This is a test of your flying speed,"
the mayor explained. "On my signal,
please fly upwards – you must be at least
one wingspan off the ground. Each fairy

must race back and forth between the tree and the stage before the next fairy in the team can start."

I am so going to let my team down, thought Pip. *I'll be last, for sure.*

When it came to her turn, she flapped her wings hard, trying her best, but soon she was being overtaken by many of the faster fairies, who flew much higher to avoid the slower, less confident fairies near the forest floor.

She was focused on fluttering her wings as hard as possible when she heard someone shout, "Watch out!"

Pip looked over her shoulder, but couldn't help but swerve at the same time. She flew into the oncoming fairy – Nutmeg – and the pair went tumbling through the air.

"I'm sorry!" Pip squeaked.

"Don't worry — it was an accident!"
Nutmeg called as the fairies fell to the
ground.

"Pip and Nutmeg, you are disqualified
for touching the ground!" croaked the
mayor. "Please leave the race!"

Pip felt awful, lowering her head as she
fluttered to the back of the tree-stump
chairs. Now two Jewel Forest teams were
out of the running. They were never
going to win the Olympics.

"I'm really sorry, Nutmeg," Pip told her friend as they sat together and watched the end of the race. The crowd's cheers got louder as three teams raced neck and neck — but it was a team from Sparkle City who won in the end, by just a wing's length.

"It's OK, I promise," said Nutmeg. "It was my fault too — I called out too late."

Pip shrugged. "I just have to face it — I'm

never going to be good at sports. I simply can't jump as high or fly as fast as everyone else."

All her forest-fairy friends did their best to reassure her, but today Pip felt completely useless. She was a terrible fairy, and didn't deserve her wings!

At least there was only one event left to go. But what would it be? Even Catkin didn't know what it was, although she was on the organizing committee.

The fairies didn't have to wait any longer to find out. The mayor hopped on to the stage again and bellowed into the microphone. "Fairies, and creatures of the forest. It is time for the final competition of the Jewel Forest Fairy Olympics! This is a special surprise, which no one has been able to prepare for – a different kind of sporting test!"

It's so quiet you could hear a dandelion seed drop, thought Pip as everyone waited to hear about the final event.

"It is called 'Reach High'," the mayor announced. "A very special prize is nestling in one of the branches of the cherry-chestnut tree," he explained, pointing to the tree at the other side of the clearing. "The aim is to reach the prize, but no wings are allowed – and no magic either! Please get into teams of no more than six."

Pip's heart sank as she waited to be picked last again, but suddenly she was surrounded by her five best friends. She frowned at Catkin, Blossom, Willa, Primrose and Nutmeg. "Don't choose me! I'll only let you down!"

Willa put an arm around Pip and gave

her a squeeze. "Of course we want you on our team, Pip. You're our friend!"

Pip gave them a small smile. "Thank you," she said softly.

"Each team will have only ten puffs of a dandelion clock to try and reach the prize," the mayor explained. "If more than one team manages it, we'll have a tiebreak."

Pip looked up at the tree, trying to see the prize – yes, she spotted something

shiny and sparkly in the branches. But it was much too high to reach – even if Willa jumped her very highest!

The first team took their places beneath the tree and the mayor waved his palm-leaf flag, signalling them to begin. But even though there were some really tall fairies who tried jumping to reach the branch, they couldn't get close. The ten puffs of the dandelion clock were soon over, and the team fluttered away, disappointed looks on their faces.

Another team flew to the tree and waited for the mayor to bring down his flag. This team tried a different tactic – they all pushed against the trunk of the tree. *They're trying to topple the prize out of the branch!* Pip realized. She glanced up at the branch, yet it hardly moved, and the prize stayed firmly stuck there. *How will anyone get it?* Pip wondered.

The next team had a clever idea. They collected leaves from the ground to throw at the branch, hoping to dislodge the prize that way. But the leaves were hard to throw and too light to reach very high, and they kept floating back down without the prize.

Pip turned to Blossom. "How in fairyland is this possible?"

Blossom raised her blonde eyebrows. "I really don't know if it is!"

But it was their turn next! The team took their places below the branch – Catkin, Blossom, Primrose, Nutmeg, Willa and Pip. *At least we're doing this together,* thought Pip. Then, as she looked at her friends, Pip had an idea.

Chapter 8

Pip beckoned her team to join her in a huddle, and she whispered her plan to them. They all nodded and smiled.

"I think that could work!" said Catkin.

"Yes, let's give it a try!" agreed Primrose.

"Ready . . . steady . . . GO!" called the mayor.

They didn't have any time to waste.

"Primrose, Blossom, Willa – can you line up at the bottom?" asked Pip.

The three fairies linked arms in a line underneath the branch.

"Now, Catkin and Nutmeg – can you climb up on to their shoulders?" Pip asked.

The two smaller fairies carefully clambered up, using their friends' linked arms as footholds. Catkin and Nutmeg straightened up with their feet on their friends' shoulders.

"OK, hold steady," said Pip. She copied what Nutmeg and Catkin had done, climbing up using her friends' linked arms and their shoulders. For once, being small was a good thing! She wouldn't be too heavy for the fairies below her.

Pip put one foot on Nutmeg's left shoulder, and one foot on Catkin's right, then slowly, carefully, straightened up. The audience cheered when they saw what Pip's team had done – they'd made a fairy pyramid!

Pip looked up – the branch was just above her head. *Phew!*

She reached up and grabbed the prize from its hiding place, and the audience clapped and squealed even louder.

"Well done!" croaked the mayor from the stage. "I think you're the smallest fairy here today, Pip, but you've shown that being tiny has its benefits!"

Pip climbed down slowly, then Nutmeg and Catkin followed. The audience kept on cheering, and before she knew what was happening, Willa had swept Pip up on to her shoulders and paraded her around. "Pi–ip!" screamed the Jewel Forest crowd. "Pi–ip!" Pip shook now and her cheeks flushed again – not in fear or embarrassment, but in surprise and delight. Her face ached from grinning so much as the friends celebrated together.

When the audience had finally quietened down, the mayor spoke again.

"So that brings the Fairy Olympics to a close, and it's time for me to announce the final scores. Dream Mountain won one event – River Rafting. Star Valley won one event – Toadstool Trampolining. Sparkle City also won one event – Fairy Relay. And Jewel Forest won two events – Branch Gymnastics and Reach High – which makes them this year's winners of the Fairy Olympics! Congratulations. . ."

The mayor's words were drowned out by the cheers in Bluebell Clearing. The Jewel Forest fairies and audience celebrated once more, hugging each other, jumping up and down, and high-fiving. In the middle of it all, Pip suddenly realized she still had the golden envelope in her hand.

She pulled her friends around her, and held out the envelope.

"I wonder what the prize will be?" said Nutmeg, jumping from foot to foot with excitement.

Pip slid a finger under the flap and took out a gold leaf sparkling with fairy-dust. On it were written just two words:

CONGRATULATIONS
VIFs

Pip frowned and turned the leaf over, but the other side was blank. "What does it mean?"

"If I can explain," croaked the mayor through the microphone, hushing the crowd. "VIF stands for Very Important

Fairy – and that's what all six of you will be tonight! You'll have the VIF table at this evening's Fairy Olympics celebration party – and be our very special guests!"

"Oh, wow!" said Willa. "I didn't know there was going to be a party!"

The fairy friends suddenly looked at Catkin, whose cheeks had flushed red. "I did, but we wanted to keep it a secret!"

"What a fantastic surprise," said Primrose. "And the perfect way to end the day!"

That evening, all the fairy competitors gathered for the party in their very best outfits. It was held in the Great Wood Hall inside the Jewel Forest Tree Palace – the perfect place for a party, with its beautiful carved wood walls, high ceiling and jewel-glass windows. As the moon shone through, the windows cast multicoloured lights into the room.

Sycamore the tree squirrel led Pip, Blossom, Catkin, Willa, Primrose and Nutmeg to the VIF table, in the very centre of the hall. It was adorned with firefly lights and jewel-flowers, and hummingbirds fluttered around it to cater for the fairies' every wish.

"May I have a forest-fruit fizz?" Pip asked one of the birds.

"Ooh, that sounds lovely – I'd like one too, please," said Blossom.

"Me too!" added Nutmeg. Eventually, all six fairies decided they'd like the delicious drink.

They sat down on silver toadstool chairs and Primrose held out her pink crystal glass. "I'd like to make a toast," she said. "To Pip, for showing us that being small can be brilliant!"

All the friends clinked their glasses together. "To Pip!" they cheered.

"For being small but mighty!" added Catkin.

Pip grinned. "And to you all, for being the best fairy friends ever!"

The forest creatures who'd watched the Fairy Olympics had agreed to be waiters and waitresses while the fairies enjoyed themselves. The fairies ate a wonderful

six-course meal prepared by the bees —
Pip's favourite part was the honey-drizzled
crumpet. It was followed by a break-
dancing beetle group and then caterpillar
karaoke. Finally, a bunny band scampered
on to the stage. They played lots of fun
forest tunes, and took special requests
from the VIFs!

"So now you're the star of the day,
have you changed
your mind about
sports?" Catkin
asked Pip as
they danced
together to
Pip's favourite
song, "Woodland
Rock".

Pip shook
her head and

shuddered. "Oh no! I'm so pleased we won the prize, but there's nothing anyone can do to persuade me to like sports!" She did a twirl and grinned. "Dancing, though – that's another matter. I could dance all night!"

And that's exactly what they did.

If you enjoyed this

Fashion Fairy Princess

book then why not visit our
magical new website!

- Explore the enchanted world of the fashion fairy princesses
- Find out which fairy princess you are
- Download sparkly screensavers
- Make your own tiara
- Colour in your own picture frame and much more!

fashionfairyprincess.com

Fashion Fairy Princess

Nutmeg

in Jewel Forest

Turn the page for a sneak peek of the next
Fashion Fairy Princess adventure...

Chapter 1

"Just one week to go until you're crowned Forest Fairy Princess, Nutmeg," said Willa, fluttering her pretty pink wings. "You must be so excited!"

"I know!" said Nutmeg, her fiery orange wings shaking as she giggled. "I can't believe I'm going to be a real princess, just like Primrose."

The two forest fairies were sitting in Nutmeg's bedroom right at the top of the Tree Palace, which stood in the heart of Jewel Forest. The forest was the biggest in fairyland. It was filled with magical trees of all shapes and sizes, covered in glittering jewels in every colour of the rainbow. The sparkliest of all the trees was the Tree Palace, an ancient pink diamond-nut tree, where Nutmeg and her big sister Princess Primrose lived with the rest of the royal family.

"What do you think?" said Willa, sliding a sapphire clip into her friend's hair.

Nutmeg inspected herself in the leaf-shaped crystal mirror and frowned. The fairy smiling back at her didn't look like her. Willa had smoothed her normally messy nut-brown hair into a shiny updo.

"Hmm, I don't know," Nutmeg said, wrinkling her freckled nose. "I look all tidy."

"That's the point," said Willa smiling at her friend. "You need to look your fairy best for the ceremony."

"It definitely needs something. Let me think," said Nutmeg, leaping up and fluttering over to an untidy stack of magazines next to her lovely but unmade four-poster bed. "I know it's here somewhere," she muttered as she examined each magazine and tossed it aside.

"Ah yes, *Sparkle Magazine*!" she exclaimed at last, pulling a twinkling packet off a bright pink magazine with a smiling fairy on the front. "I really wanted to try this! I think it'll look great."

"Glimmerberry jewel gel?" said Willa, reading the small packet. "I don't know, Nutmeg. Don't you think jewel gel is a bit funky for the ceremony?"

"Perhaps," said Nutmeg, her eyes twinkling with fun, "but let's give it a try anyway."

Willa squeezed the sparkly gel into her tiny hands and spread it evenly through Nutmeg's hair.

"Let me have a go," said Nutmeg, pushing her fingers through her hair until it was all standing up straight. "There," she said when she had finished. "What do you think?"

Willa laughed. "Nutmeg! That's brilliant," she said, touching Nutmeg's hair, which was now styled into shimmering spikes. "I can't imagine what everyone would say if you wore it like that for the ceremony."

"I know," said Nutmeg, "it would be very funny, but I wouldn't dare."

"What is it you have to do for the ceremony?" asked Willa, more seriously. "Don't you have to recite a pledge?"

"Yes, but that's not all!" said Nutmeg excitedly. "First I need to look like a princess, which is what you're helping me with now," she said, giggling at her hair in the mirror. "I recite the princess pledge after I perform a special dance. Then everyone sings the forest fairy sacred song and Father puts the crown on my head. After that I'll be a real-life princess."

"Wow!" said Willa, "that sounds like an awful lot of work. Do you know the pledge by heart?"

"Oh yes!" said Nutmeg confidently. "Well, almost. I'll recite it for you."

Nutmeg stood up, gave a tiny cough to clear her throat, then began:

"All forest fairies and creatures who live

Among deep roots to branches high
I swear to . . . something,
    something . . . home
And sing loudly at the, um,
    something sky."

"Are you sure that's how it goes?"
asked Willa, frowning. "Perhaps it just
sounded different when Primrose said it at
her crowning ceremony."

"Well," said Nutmeg quickly, "I've still
got loads of time to learn it properly.
Would you like to see my dance?"

"Oh yes!" said Willa, fluttering on to
the bed to give her friend some room.
"Primrose's dance was so beautiful. Will
you do the same one?"

"Er . . . not exactly the same, no,"
said Nutmeg as she fluttered over to her
enchanted wooden music box and chose

the song she wanted to play.

Nutmeg took her position in the centre of the room and began to dance. She started well, twirling and fluttering in time to the music, but then she forgot what she was supposed to do next.

"Do I leap or twirl here?" she asked herself, swaying on the spot for a moment. "Well, I have to do something." She grinned, then began to scamper across the room just like one of the candy tufted tree squirrels that lived in Jewel Forest.

Willa burst out laughing.

Nutmeg stopped and started fluttering and pecking around the room like a little bird.

"Oh, Nutmeg! Stop!" Willa howled with laughter until her sides ached. "Please! I . . . hahaha . . . can't . . . breathe."

Nutmeg smiled. She loved having fun with her fairy friends.

And I've got plenty of time to get ready for the ceremony, she thought, before slipping on the packet of glimmerberry jewel gel and tumbling to the floor with a crash.

At that moment, the door to Nutmeg's room swung open and there stood Princess Primrose who, unlike Willa and Nutmeg, wasn't smiling or laughing.

"Nutmeg!" said Primrose. "What *are* you doing?"

Get creative with the fashion fairy princesses in
these magical sticker-activity books!